Forest
of Fire

BLANCA P. MORA PRATT

Enjoy the book

Thank you,

Blanca

DEDICATION

To the wild.

CONTENTS

Acknowledgments   i

1   A New Stable   Pg 1

2   The First Lesson   Pg 5

3   A Call from the Wild   Pg 9

4   A Mysterious Dream   Pg 13

5   A Brewing Storm   Pg 17

6   The Daring Escape   Pg 20

7   A Dangerous Wood   Pg 25

8   A Friendly Explanation   Pg 29

9   The Wild Challenge   Pg 34

10   The Painful Truth   Pg 38

11   A Happy Reunion   Pg 44

12   A Risky Plan   Pg 48

13   Moments Before   Pg 51

14   The Humans Attack   Pg 55

15   The Forest of Fire   Pg 59

16   Home   Pg 63

ACKNOWLEDGMENTS

Lots of thanks to my mother for the illustrations and formatting, and my father for reading through my book and supporting me.

HORSES

Stellar – Black appaloosa mare with white spots on her hind legs and dark brown eyes.

Tallulah – Coffee and white dappled Icelandic horse mare with striped hair and mango orange eyes.

Rose – Cream and white-haired thoroughbred mare with dark brown eyes.

Blaze – Black and white trakehner stallion and black eyes.

Vera – Chocolate brown Irish cob mare with knee-length hair and a white muzzle with hazel eyes.

Xanthia – Pale, sandy mare with grey-ish brown-ish hair and icy eyes.

Pyralis – Chestnut stallion with white muzzle, white legs, and dark brown eyes.

Amin – Muscular vanilla stallion with caramel hair and crystal blue eyes.

Brone – Lean, tan stallion with black legs, black hair, and sky-blue eyes.

Demetra – Light grey mare with stormy grey spots, black hair, and jungle green eyes.

Peanut – Dark brown and white dappled Icelandic horse stallion with striped hair.

Cecilia – Blind, misty grey foal with milky eyes.

Kafe – Very dark brown mare with black hair and brown eyes.

Kosmos – Lighter brown mare with black hair and brown eyes.

Arcadia – Pale grey mare with black hair and dark green eyes.

Myra – Peanut brown mare with vanilla hair and caramel eyes.

FOREST OF FIRE

1

A NEW STABLE

Stellar's eyes slowly opened. The stable windows were foggy from the thick, cold air. Rolling green hills continued for miles in the distance outside. She searched the feeding bag with her muzzle, but all that was left were the fine wheat flakes that fell to the ground. She rubbed her chin on the shaky wooden gates as she huffed in frustration. She was up early, and the only light in the sky was the pale, soft sunrise. Stellar peered at each of the other stalls, but no faces were to be seen.

Her black tail nervously swept the air. "Hello?" Stellar whispered. She had just moved to a different stable that night, and she hadn't met anyone yet in this new barn.

It felt exactly like moving to a new school. As something stirred behind the stall that faced her, its gates crashed. Then a pair of alarmed orange eyes glanced over at her. Stellar snorted in amusement as their face gradually became clear.

A thick, snow-white forelock that flowed between their pointed ears belonged to that of an Icelandic horse. She had a petite body with fine brown dots freckling her white flank, and a mane of rich brown and white hair. "Hi," Stellar gulped.

The pony's eyes sparkled, blooming mango orange.

"Hi!" She whinnied, "You must be new around here."

"Yes, I am," Stellar replied with a sigh of relief, "I came from Yellowmoor Stables."

The horse with spots grimaced. "Isn't that being rebuilt into a mall?" she grumbled. Stellar's brown eyes grew The Icelandic horse circled in her stall and said, "That's likely why you got moved here, but anyways, welcome to Puma Riding Camp!"

"Riding camp," Stellar echoed, "This isn't where humans learn how to ride horses, right?" she sniffed. From the opposite side of the stable, she examined the stranger's face. After a little pause, the pony answered, "Yes, it is. They adore horses! They love the ponies the most," they added, with a tone of bragging, "However, I can offer you some advice!"

Stellar answered glumly, "If it's advice on how to scare humans away, I'm all ears."

The pony's eyes sparkled with mirth. "My name is Tallulah. What's yours?"

"Stellar," she replied. Straining her ears, Stellar could hear thudding against the wooden floor. It became more louder until...

"Look! They're here!" Tallulah exclaimed with joy. Stellar watched in horror as small humans wearing rose gold coats entered the stables one by one. They all had their hair pinned up and long, dark scarlet boots covered their feet. Stellar observed the group of three girls gathered in front of Tallulah's stall. They chittered angrily among themselves, putting their small hands on their hips, and pointing at the speckled pony. A girl with brown hair and large blue eyes looked at Stellar up and down. Stellar felt a chill go down her back. One of the humans reached over the gates to stroke Tallulah's back. *What are they doing?* Stellar wondered, *and why isn't Tallulah running away?*

As if reading her thoughts, Tallulah's warm tangerine gaze turned to Stellar. "It's fine! I thought you came fro a stable, not the wild!" Tallulah blinked. *I am from a stable*, Stellar concluded sourly, *a neglected one.* Suddenly, a slender woman with streaming red hair burst into the stables.

She pointed at the three girls standing in front of Tallulah's stall, her eyes wild. "Julie, Anne, and Millie!" She called. The three girls froze, startled. "Stop arguing about Tallulah! Two of you pick a different horse!" Two of the girls searched the other stalls, jealously looking back at Tallulah and the blonde-haired girl that remained. *Which one of them will ride me?* Stellar pondered curiously.

2

THE FIRST LESSON

Five horses lined up in front of the human as they gently trotted out of the stables. A black and white Trakehner with its head bowed elegantly and tail whipping in the icy breeze was noticeably comparable to Stellar's dusty black flank and eyes prickling with anxiety. A Morgan stood next to him, with a flank that was a light tan hue and a sugar-icing white mane. Her snout was scrunched up in disgust when she met Stellar's gaze. The last horse was an Irish Cob that was dark brown with a silky, black mane that flowed halfway down her legs. She had a rosy muzzle and a white blaze building from her snout to her forehead. The ginger-haired woman stated, "I'd like to welcome you to our newest horse, Stellar."

Even the horses had a glance at Stellar when her name was called out. "*Ooo!*" The younger humans chorused.

The woman added, "She is an Appaloosa from Yellowmoor Stables."

"That's Kat," an excited voice whispered in her ear. It was Tallulah. "She's the teacher of Puma Riding Camp."

Stellar's ears pricked inquisitively. "Teacher?" she gruffed.

"Teacher," Tallulah affirmed. "The girl on top of you is Tan. She's really nice, the nicest here." Stellar glanced up at the girl on her back. She was watching Kat intently as the adult yammered about safety rules. "To the jumping course!" Kat ordered, a puff of cold air fuming from her mouth. She jogged off into the morning mist, and Stellar and the others followed.

A minute later, they were lined up in a sandy clearing where pink poles balanced on bricks. A stone of anxiety weighed heavily in Stellar's stomach.

She hadn't jumped before, especially not with a human on her back. She calmed herself down with a flick of her ear. "Julie, go first!" Kat called to the black-haired girl on the Trakehner horse. The black and white horse trotted forward, his head held low and his braided tail drifting in the breeze.

Suddenly, he picked up speed and they both jumped gracefully over one of the poles, until they jumped over all of them and landed neatly beside Kat. "Next, Anne."

Kat ordered. Stellar's chin lifted as Tallulah walked slowly to the first pole. Swiftly, she leapt over the pole in one desperate leap and landed onto the other side. A wave of sand rose from her hooves as she jumped over another pole, and then the last few. "Tan, please," Kat called whilst clapping.

Tan? Stellar thought, her throat dry. *It's my turn!*

Stellar felt a soft hand pat her neck. "Let's do this," Tan's voice whispered behind her. Stellar trotted forward anxiously, and once the intimidating pole drew nearer, she jumped as high as she could, scrunching her eyes shut. Suddenly, she felt the sand beneath her hooves and opened her eyes. She'd done it! Stellar galloped forward to the next pole and kicked off the ground, landing firmly onto the other side. She swerved over to the last pole, her heart racing. She held her breath and jumped. The pink pole clashed against her leg painfully and Stellar let out a neigh of fright. They both rolled over the other side. Tan was sniffling whilst staggering to her feet. "Tan! Stellar! Are you alright?" Kat shouted frantically, sprinting towards them.

Stellar's legs were bruised where the poles had hit her, but it was nothing compared to the blood roaring in her ears. She nosed Tan nervously, and then let out a snort as Tan stroked her muzzle gently. "Are you okay?" Tan rasped, still petting Stellar on the snout. "Class dismissed," Kat said, taking Stellar's reins and leading her outside of the jumping course. "Take the horses to their stalls!' The teacher called behind her shoulder as they left. Stellar's head hung low, her flank hot with shame. She passed the other horses. "You're wild," the palomino scowled in her ear as she passed.

3

A CALL FROM THE WILD

The five horses were out in the paddocks, grazing quietly as the oily sun slowly wafted towards the horizon. Stellar stuck close to Tallulah the whole afternoon. "Hi," the lean, inky horse greeted Stellar with a dip of his head, "Who are you?"

"Stellar," Stellar replied, lifting her muzzle from the lawn. "From Yellowmoor stables."

"I am Blaze, and that is Rose and Vera," The stallion introduced, his ears pointed to the horses grazing behind him. He gave a snort of disgust as he gazed down at the grass, and then over his shoulder. "The grass is better over our side," Blaze informed, "Would you care to join us?"

"She wouldn't," Tallulah answered protectively,

stepping forward. The pony's ears flattened. Tallulah's eyes sparkled guiltily as she looked back at Stellar. "Sorry," Stellar shuffled her hooves, "maybe another time."

Blaze nodded with a glance at Tallulah. Was that anger in his eyes? He trotted back to the other side of the paddock, where Rose lifted her head and murmured something to him. Blaze's eyes widened. "I'm going to explore," Stellar grunted, flicking her tail. She trotted further down the paddocks, to the setting sun.

Suddenly, a sharp breeze made Stellar stumble and crash against the fences that stopped her from entering the forest. "Ouch!" Stellar gasped, and the wind howled, like crying in sorrow. *It's like telling me to go to the forest,* Stellar dreamed. Tallulah stepped beside her. "Are you okay?" She frowned.

"Yep, just-just the wind!" Stellar neighed over the harsh breeze. Her mind was whirling. Tallulah shrugged and trotted off. Her stomach clenched as she went back to grazing.

The next morning, Stellar was having her second lesson: Racing. *This is going to be easy!* Stellar thought in triumph, as Anne, the girl who rode Tallulah the day before, clipped a bridle onto her snout. Her eyes sparkled in excitement as she was led out into the racing course. There were white fences lined in an oval shape, and the ground was dusty and orange. The warm sun peeked through the grumbling clouds.

"Okay," Kat's voice broke the silence. Everyone straightened up and listened. "Remember, you cannot cheat," she counted on her fingers, "You *must* be careful, AND you have to work with your horse!"

Anne nodded eagerly. She was squeezing Stellar's bridle like a monkey, her entire face flushing red. Kat held up a checkered flag that wafted in the wind, as if waving at them. "On your marks…" she called. Stellar felt like she could shoot all the way up to the moon. "Get steady…"

"GO!"

Stellar galloped as fast as she could. At first, she was in the league, her black hair firing out behind her, but then Rose sprinted in front of her, and then Blaze. She breathed heavily and galloped harder, but her hooves started to ache.

Anne wacked her reins against her shoulders crossly. "Hurry up! Go, go, go!" she shrieked excitedly. Suddenly Stellar caught a glimpse of Tallulah hurrying beside her, her belly almost touching the rusty ground and her coffee-brown tail streaming out behind her.

The finish line was only several horse-lengths away. She could hear her heart thudding in her chest now, as Tallulah fell behind again.

Stellar could spot Vera galloping behind her.

Her hair was a rich brown stream bursting into a waterfall.

4

A MYSTERIOUS DREAM

Although the Irish cob was slow now, she was picking up speed, her hooves thundering against the floor. Stellar needed to pick up her pace.

She galloped forward with all her strength, bursting past Rose, and heading towards the finish line. Finally - the moment she'd been waiting for! Although Blaze had already come first, she'd come second, and at least that was better than third, or last! "Woohoo!" Anne shouted behind her. Stellar had skidded to a halt past the finish line.

Her heart slowed to a calm, steady beat as she caught her breath. Her hooves were aching as if they had been set on fire! Tallulah and Vera halted beside her, gasping for breath. Stellar's ears fell back as she realised, her friend and Vera had come third, and in this case, last.

She frowned. "You did great," Stellar nudged Tallulah playfully.

"Thanks," Tallulah grunted. The clouds had parted away, and a new ray of light showered down on the horses, warming their backs. Kat caught up to them with a bright smile. "Well done!" she commented, "Let's all take the horses to the stables for a rest."

"Yes please," Stellar huffed, remembering the aches and strains in her legs. Tallulah giggled. "Can't wait!"

She was having a dream. Stellar stood in darkness, but wherever she stepped, her hooves splashed in an inky liquid. There was no stable, no sky, no grass, no movement. It was all black. Suddenly, as she walked onwards, she noticed a forest drawing closer and closer to her. Birds were tweeting in the rich canopy. New shoots were seen on the stems. The trees stood like soldiers, gazing down at Stellar as she explored the wilderness. Gradually the forest thinned out until she reached the end, and into the black mist again.

Her hooves splish-sploshed through the pitch-black. As she turned around to glimpse one last look at the forest, she could see a big, yellow engine thundering through it, swallowing up whatever was in its path. It had a big, sharp hand that ripped the trees free from the earth and threw them away like a feather. Suddenly, the canopy burst into flames. Neighs of fright echoed in the air.

Stellar's heart was racing as she turned backwards, into the woods. She could spot wild horses galloping over the bushes in terror. There was one muscular horse, a pale vanilla and strong, like a lion. He had blue eyes as clear as crystal.

His caramel mane was streaming and blazing out behind him as he reared onto his hind legs. "COME BACK!" he demanded the wild horses. "They will come to us soon!"

Stellar opened her deep brown eyes. She gazed out the sunlit window, out at the green hills that unfolded like a wide carpet into the distance. Tallulah's ear twitched. "What are you doing?" she neighed, leaning over the gates. Stellar pivoted to face her. Her eyes were dark but brimmed with interest. "What would it be like, living in the wild?" Stellar pondered quietly. She turned her head back to look out at the paddocks and woods.

"Oh," Tallulah breathed, "I'm not so sure. You'd have to ask *them.*" she replied with a snort. She peered at Stellar with worry when she didn't answer, "Are you okay?"

Stellar whinnied, "I'm fine!" but a moment later, a flash of her nightmare snared her sight. "I-I feel like something's wrong," Stellar stammered. She glanced at Tallulah's bewildered face, "I think the wild horses are in danger." Tallulah's face froze. Her eyes shadowed. Then salty tears ran down her muzzle. Stellar fell silent

15

before she realised Tallulah was crying in laughter. "What?" Tallulah snickered, "Wild horses - in danger?!"

5

A BREWING STORM

And then she started to laugh, too. They laughed until their throats felt dry and their voices were wheezing, and until Rose lifted her head and told them to shush. "I know it sounds crazy," Stellar said at last, "But it's true. Yesterday the wind almost made me fly over the fences. I wasn't hallucinating, Tallulah. It wanted me to go the forest!"

Tallulah's tail whipped the air. "Real..." she echoed. Her eyes were still twinkling with amusement. "And," Stellar continued, "I had a dream. I found a forest, and then it set on fire, and there was a giant yellow machine-thing, and then there was a giant horse telling all these wild horses that someone was coming!"

Tallulah huffed. "Don't get too hyped up. What if you're wrong?"

"Please," Stellar replied frustratedly. "We need to save the wild horses *now!*"

"Dreams aren't real, Stellar," Tallulah replied quietly. "You should just forget about it and wonder around the paddocks or eat apples. Like a normal horse!"

"It wasn't a dream," Stellar insisted, her eyes prickling with impatience. "It was a message."

Suddenly, the stable doors swung open and clashed against the wooden walls, making Stellar jump. Kat was standing there, her sapphire eyes sparkling. "Let's take you all to the paddock!"

As she led the five horses to the paddock, Stellar kept trying to convince Tallulah that they had to save the wild horses. But most of the time she was ignored. "Please, Tallulah. Horses are in danger! What if this is real and we're just standing here, eating grass?" Stellar pleaded, nudging her friend on the side. The pony just gruffed and picked up her pace.

My dream is real. I can feel it, Stellar shivered, *why have I been given this message if it's not real? And that breeze- it was leading me somewhere! Maybe it was leading me to the wild horses! Maybe the forest was telling me to come to it!*

"Watch it!" Rose snapped as Stellar bumped her shoulder into her flank. "Sorry," Stellar muttered with a dip of her head. She didn't have time for Rose's sourness. She needed to find out more about her dream!

As they were grazing on the lawn a few minutes later, Stellar was still thinking. *How can I make Tallulah believe me?* She cleared out a patch of grass and moved somewhere else where fresh, new shoots awaited her. *If she doesn't believe me, I can just go by myself!*

"Hi," Tallulah's small voice whispered in her ear. Stellar glanced at the pony now grazing beside her. "Hey," she replied awkwardly. "Do you believe me now?"

Tallulah sighed. "I-I've been thinking about it, I guess," she murmured, her voice muffled out by a big batch of grass in her mouth. "And I do know that some wild horses live there, in the woods beyond the hills." "Oh," Stellar's eyes widened. "Really?"

"Yes," Tallulah confirmed. "They roam the woods of Silverberry."

"Are you sure they're the right ones?" Stellar quizzed, lifting her head.

"No," Tallulah snorted, her ears flattening. "But if you tell me what the horses in your dream look like," she added, "then I might be right. And we need to save them."

6

A DARING ESCAPE

After Tallulah had finally believed Stellar, Stellar had been telling her all about her dream and the purple mouse, in more detail. "It happened here," Stellar told Tallulah. The sun was sinking through the horizon, pale and vague through the cold, twilight mist. Tallulah's eyes brightened. "Will the breeze come again?"

"Um," Stellar muttered. "I'm not sure."

Tallulah narrowed her eyes in suspicion. "I'm not lying!" Stellar promised.

"Then how will we find the herd's home if it's not there?" Tallulah frowned. Stellar looked down at her hooves. "I'm not so sure." Her eyes fixed on the sunset.

"What did the horses in your dream look like?" Tallulah

questioned eagerly. "Did one of them look like me?"

Stellar recalled her thoughts and her dream. Then a butterfly of hope fluttered in her stomach. "Yes, actually," she neighed, "and there was a grey dappled one, too!"

"Demetra!" Tallulah squealed in delight. Despite her joy, Stellar was still curious. "How do you know the wild horses?" she asked.

"Oh," Tallulah grunted, "Peanut used to be a horse in Puma Riding Camp. But after he met Demetra, he decided to become one!"

Suddenly, Rose trotted up behind them. Her eyes were rolling. "Wooow, what a *romantic* story," she laughed faintly. Then her eyes glared at Tallulah. "He didn't 'escape' into the wild with Demetra, Tallulah. The wild horses kidnapped him and killed him deep in the Silverberry woods."

Stellar shivered, and her eyes widened with horror. *Are wild horses really like that?* Tallulah didn't seem convinced. "You're just trying to scare us," she spat, lashing her plumed tail in Rose's face. "But they even told me that they were going to run away." Rose scoffed and turned away in the direction of Vera. She gossiped in her ear, but she completely ignored Rose.

She turned back to Tallulah. "Let's wait for the wind to

lead us."

They fidgeted for a while, under the melting sun. Stellar's legs were aching, and her hooves felt heavy. She was about to give up before she felt a breeze touch her back. Leaves swirled and danced in the direction of the forest. And then, Stellar realised, it was there again.

"Tallulah!" she neighed in delight. "It's here! Come on!" She chased the whistling wind down the paddocks, and Tallulah caught up with her. Her eyes were wide in excitement. "If all of this is a prank, I'm going to kill you!" she snorted.

The leaves pranced and pirouetted, in the direction of Silverberry. Stellar's heart drummed. "It's going to the forest!"

"Scared?" Tallulah teased. Suddenly, the pony did a run-up and sailed over the fence. She skidded to a halt on the other side, spraying grass and mud behind her. Stellar's ears perked up. "You're really going to - to leave this place?" she tilted her head.

Tallulah glanced over her shoulder at her friend. "Isn't that what you've been trying to convince me to do for ages?!"

"I thought you'd be, well, sad…" Stellar began, before she realised that the leaves were almost out of sight. "Never mind!" she gasped.

Her ears flattened, and she drew back from the fence. She leapt out and flew over the fence in one big jump and rolled onto the other side and staggered to her hooves. "Let's go!" she whinnied.

7

A DANGEROUS WOOD

Stellar shivered from snout to tail-tip. Looming, wooden soldiers blocked out the sky with bustling, copper leaves. A thick layer of mud caked the forest floor. It was deep, cold, and gurgling. "Can we go back now?" Stellar joked, and Tallulah swung her head to stare at Stellar with glimmering eyes. "Ha-ha." She mumbled, with a nervous twitch of her ear.

Stellar could tell they were both scared. The air was clammy and stale, and she felt packed in by all the weeds tangling her legs and the bushes crowding. Screeching noises echoed in the canopy. "How can horses live here?" Stellar pondered, snorting in disgust. "It's terrible!"

"Told you so," Tallulah frowned. Dead leaves were

strewn across the ground, ivy choked the ancient trees, and something in the bushes quivered. Stellar looked down. She could see footprints in the mud. Not just hers and Tallulah's, but weirdly shaped ones, with an upside-down heart in the middle and four dots surrounding it. Grey fur stuck out of the crawling brown. Stellar's stomach clenched. "Tallulah!" she called, and the pony hurried back to her side. "Look."

Tallulah gazed down at the pawprints, and then took a sniff from the fluff. Her eyes prickled with fear. "Wolves," the pony breathed. Before they knew it, a big, matted wolf leapt out from the bushes. It arched it's back and a deep growl brewed in its throat. Tallulah and Stellar started to back away.

"We want no trouble, doggy," Stellar laughed faintly, "He-he."

"We taste terrible, anyway," Tallulah joined in, her voice shaky, "ew," she shivered, "even thinking about it, I get dizzy!"

The wolf pricked its ears and drooped its shoulders. It sniffed the air curiously. Stellar beckoned for Tallulah and they shuffled away into the bushes slowly, their sight gradually becoming clouded by leaves. Suddenly, something cracked. A broken twig laid beneath Stellar's hoof.

The wolf howled in a deep tone. Several other wolves

cried out excitedly and the ground started to shake. "RUN!" Tallulah neighed. They galloped away into the forest, struggling through thistle, and stumbling over weeds. Stellar remembered the race. This reminded her of it.

A neigh echoed in the forest and the wolves halted in alarm. The crisp leaves on the ground danced as the sound of galloping got louder. "A wild horse!" Tallulah's voice squealed in relief nearby. Stellar pivoted to look behind her and froze. Between the trees, she could spot a skinny horse rearing onto their hooves, and the sound of fearful barks. And the wolves vanished into the bushes.

"Thank you!" Tallulah cried and she treaded over the bushes, over to the mysterious horse. Stellar tensed. "Tallulah," she grimaced. She stayed in her spot behind a thorn bush, peering over at Tallulah and the wild horse. Her tail twitched nervously.

The wild horse was a pale sandy colour, with loose strands of silky white hair rippling down their neck. Her face was long, and ribs jutted out from her sides. Her cold grey eyes glared at Tallulah. "Who are you?" she scowled. Tallulah quivered. Before she could answer, the mare reared onto her hooves. "You reek of human!" she neighed.

Tallulah's ears flattened in terror.

Stellar trampled towards them, kicking a twig out of the way. Her eyes brimmed with guilt. "We want no trouble," Stellar grunted, taking a step towards the horse. The stranger's eyes narrowed as she continued, "We- "

"Are you a Brone, or an Amin?" the horse interrupted. Her eyes fixed on Stellar and Tallulah, like two grey flames that illuminated her face. When Stellar and Tallulah froze, puzzled, she repeated: "Brone or Amin!"

"Whatever that is, we don't want trouble," Stellar huffed. And then, the horse neighed in warning.

"No!" Tallulah cried out, but it was too late. The mare reared up and hit Stellar hard in the head with her hoof. Her mane streamed out behind her as she pummelled Stellar's flank. Stellar coughed, pain swivelling through her body. "Ow!" she gasped and crashed down to the ground. The wild horse stared down at her. "That was a test," she smiled.

8

A FRIENDLY EXPLANATION

"I am Xanthia," the mustang explained, helping Stellar up. "You two must be from somewhere else. You trudge through the forests like angry bears."

Stellar was still sore from the bruises on her side. She snorted. *Why did I have to be the one getting kicked? What is her problem?!*

Xanthia recognised her expression. "If you were a wild horse you would understand," and then her icy gaze flicked to Tallulah. "You are domestic horses, aren't you?"

Tallulah and Stellar nodded. "Can I ask you a question?" Tallulah neighed nervously.

"You just did," Xanthia grunted.

"Who are Brone and Amin?" Tallulah asked. Xanthia's gaze softened. "They are our ancestors," she replied, "they are brothers."

"They separate the good and the evil - they are complete opposites. The wild horses used to live in fear, and they used to not know how to scare wolves or how to fight bears. They died quickly, and there was no offspring. The herd was under great danger of extinction."

"Brone and Amin were given a quest, to return the heart of the forest: they would travel to the very top of the mountains, and they would speak to their wise sister, Fauna. Fauna said: 'You must come up with ways to fight, to rule the forest. But not just the strength you need- you also need agility, and wisdom. You need to know how to hide, to sprint, to heal. I give you this knowledge so you can teach our herd the ways.' So, Amin and Brone returned with the heart and taught the herd strength, agility, and wisdom. But all Brone wanted, was strength. He said: 'The strongest have fought hard to have what they have earned. The weakest have nothing left but sorrow, pain, and drained energy. We shall only keep the strongest, and for the weakest: they shall die in pain and live to suffer.'"

"Half of the herd agreed: and for the other half, they stayed in the forest with Amin. They said: 'You are only strong if you care for the weak. With care, you are stronger in the heart, and in your brain. But with no care, you are only strong with your anger and your muscle; your brain will be devoured by helpless fury!' So, then they agreed, that whoever had care would stay in the forest with Amin, and whoever had no care, would leave with Brone. We do not know where they have gone, after that."

"So finally, we have a law. If you say you are with Amin, you are trustworthy, kind, and faithful. If you say you are with Brone, you are brainless, heartless and blood thirsty."

"Wow," Tallulah breathed. "Can't we just say we're with Amin, even though we're with Brone?" she tilted her head.

"You are?" Xanthia froze.

"No!" Tallulah and Stellar panicked.

"Oh," Xanthia chuckled, "then you wouldn't say that. Horses with Brone stay with Brone. They think the horses of Amin are stupid. WE think they're stupid. They couldn't betray their leader like that." "I think they're stupid, too," Tallulah gruffed, and they all laughed.

"So, you are part of a herd, you say?" Stellar butted in. Xanthia turned to her. "Yeah, so?" she grunted. Stellar pricked her ears. This might be a horse part of the herd in her dream!

Talking about my dream, Stellar thought, *is 'Amin' the big horse?* "What does Amin look like?" Stellar quizzed, her tail whipping the air in excitement. Xanthia's eyes glittered in surprise, and then she snorted.

9

A WILD CHALLENGE

"He is rumoured to be made of purple jewels, but the eldest of the herd describe him to be a light vanilla with caramel hair." Xanthia described as they trotted through the whispering trees. Then she shook her head, and added, "but we can never be sure. Amin died around 40 years ago."

"Oh," Tallulah huffed, sounding disappointed. *That is the same horse in my dream!* Stellar realised. *But who did that breeze-magic thingy?* They continued to walk, but Stellar was sizzling with energy. All her questions were brewing in her head like a big storm, striking with big questions, and some completely stupid. She was afraid that she was asking too much of Xanthia, maybe she could just say nothing and find out herself. The clouds in her head fogged her sight until all she could do was -

"Can Amin like- affect the wind?" Stellar's voice broke out awkwardly. Xanthia whipped around, surprise glittering in her eyes. And then they grew deep, and cold, like the crawling mud beneath them. "How do you know- "she snapped, but before she could finish, a chestnut red horse leapt neatly over the thistle beyond them. He halted in front of Xanthia, his cheeks flushed red and his eyes wild, as if he had been running.

"Xanthia! We need you back, Arcadia and Myra- "and then he looked at Tallulah and Stellar. He lashed his tail and opened his mouth.

"Long story, Pyralis," Xanthia butted in, her voice silky and her eyes narrowed calmly, "bring me to Arcadia and Myra," Xanthia ordered, glancing over her shoulder at Stellar and Tallulah. "They will come, too," she decided. The chestnut stallion's gaze was hard for a moment, but then he nodded swiftly and disappeared through the trees.

Xanthia smirked at Stellar and Tallulah in amusement. "Let's see what domestic horses can do," she neighed and galloped after the stallion.

Stellar did not know why she had bothered to follow, or what her life would be like if she hadn't. But she did anyway and struggled very badly. Stellar's hooves scratched the thorns as she leapt over the thistle bush. Xanthia and Pyralis were already far ahead, but if she kept her pace, she would still be able to follow them.

She trampled over the weeds and crushed the stinging nettles with triumph. But as Xanthia dodged and weaved confidently through the bushes and trees, Stellar felt bad.

So, she managed to skim past the bushes, and ran lightly on the squelching mud. Leaves crunched behind her, and Tallulah shot her a puzzled glance. Stellar just grinned.

Up ahead, a deep, cold stream weaved through the trees. It twinkled in the daylight, and slim shadows flickered underneath the mirroring surface. Stellar hesitated as they drew close. Xanthia and Pyralis leapt over swiftly and disappeared behind a big oak. Stellar, determinedly, trailed after. Her and Tallulah did a run-up and flew over the river. But halfway across, they both crashed into it. Stellar's head sunk underneath the ice-cold water and fish darted madly back in alarm.

Stellar tried to pull herself up, to find the waves dunk her head underwater again. The fierce cold bit into her flailing legs. Her struggles felt weaker. Her lungs were burning for air. Her shoulders were starting to relax, and she let herself sink. Suddenly jaws closed around her neck, and she was yanked free from the darkness, back into the glaring sun. Tallulah laid her down beside the riverbank, catching her breath. Warm stone heated Stellar's back, and she staggered to her hooves.
Her flank was damp, and her hair was dripping, wet, like seaweed. She shuddered and noticed Tallulah's laughing

face. And the next thing Stellar knew, they both laughed. Xanthia snorted, "Great swimmers!" and she galloped off. Stellar and Tallulah followed excitedly.

10

THE PAINFUL TRUTH

As Stellar and Tallulah stepped into Xanthia and Pyralis' home, they were not surprised. The entrance was lined with ash and crippled heather. Charcoal-black branches swayed and creaked overhead, as if groaning in pain. The mud underfoot was churned up and stained a cold red. Stellar and Tallulah exchanged anxious glances.

"Pyralis," Xanthia grunted, "What is wrong with Arcadia?" her voice wobbled when she said the word 'Arcadia'. "She coughed more today," Pyralis reported, his eyes clouding, "this afternoon she fainted, and then woke up sobbing that her lungs were…" his voice faded as he ducked beneath some dangling ivy.

Stellar and Tallulah hung back, and they turned to each other. "Think you found the right herd?" Tallulah questioned. "Yes," Stellar exhaled. "Yes, and I've got lots of questions." Tallulah laughed faintly, then sighed. "These horses are in great danger," before she could say more, Xanthia's voice called from behind the bushes and ivy. "Come on in, human pets!" she teased.

As Stellar stepped through the ivy, she was pleasantly surprised. The sky was smothered with entwined twigs and sheltering leaves, and so were on either side, forming a giant, leafy den.

There was no mud here, but it was sandy, and moss nests lay ahead of her, lined with pigeon feathers and fluff.

At the far end of the den, there was a rock shaft and inside the shadowed holes it held were bundles of leaves and juicy berries. But apart from the welcoming herbs and warm sand, the air was hot, stale, and thick with sickness. In one of the nests lay a tired mare who seemed to be so skinny her ribs showed in her sides, and her legs were as thin as paper.

She was a pale grey with a darker mane, and her eyes were dark green and weak from exhaustion. She had dark patches under her eyes and seemed to be staring out at the wilderness beyond, curling her spindly black tail over her legs.

In a nest behind was a palomino, who was chestnut with whisky vanilla hair. Her cheeks were much softer, and her caramel eyes were fiery, still holding a light. She seemed much plumper and her ears twitched with boredom. "Can I leave now? I feel great," she got to her hooves before anyone could answer.

"No," Pyralis' voice made Stellar jump. "You are not fit enough to go outside yet, Myra. If you suddenly burst in energy now, your coughing will only get worse."

"But she needs to exercise to become stronger," Xanthia argued, scaring Pyralis out of his pelt. "How will she ever be strong enough to fight off the coughing, if she sits in a nest all day not moving?"

Pyralis shuffled his hooves. "Fine. Alright. I'll take her outside for a few minutes," and the two horses disappeared out of the exit.

Xanthia sighed and turned to the grey mare. "How are you doing, Arcadia?"

Arcadia slowly craned her neck to look up at the sandy horse. And then she fell into a pout of ragged coughing that echoed in the den. Stellar drew back and flattened her ears. When Arcadia was finished coughing, she rasped: "Fire! Everywhere!" and she started coughing again.

"Huh," Xanthia twitched her ear and turned to Stellar and Tallulah. "I suggest you leave and hang out with Pyralis and Myra. They're just outside, I bet. Pyralis won't take his little sister too far away from her nest."

Nodding, Stellar and Tallulah stepped out of the shadows of the den. Stellar was relieved to get away from the stench as fresh air buffeted her face. Not far off Pyralis was rolling up some moss into the shape of a ball. Next to him, Myra had her snout tilted to the sky and her eyes squinting, against the bright sun.

Their voices were too quiet to hear, but as they drew closer the two wild horses' voices became clearer.

"...After I'm finished, we can play throw and catch with this ball," Pyralis was saying.

Myra exhaled. "I wish I could tell my past self not to breath that smoke," her voice was cracked and sorrowful. Then her back arched, and she coughed.

"What's past is in the past," Pyralis reminded her, looking up from the moss he was fidgeting with. "Sometimes it's good to get sick, so you know how to fight it off next time it happens," he pointed out, and then picked up the ball of moss. "Done!" he whinnied.

"Hi," Stellar interrupted. The siblings turned to look at them. "Hello?" Pyralis fumbled, his voice muffled out by the moss. Before it got awkward, Tallulah stepped forward, suddenly excited.

"I am Peanut's sister, Tallulah," Tallulah greeted. "I'd like to know where Peanut is," and then she added, "oh, and Demetra!"

Pyralis shot her a look of suspicion, then shrugged when Myra nodded and instructed, "Of course! Just keep walking straight and then turn right by the ash tree, and you'll find Peanut and Demetra. I think some others are there, too."

Tallulah dipped her head gratefully. "Come on, Stellar! You're going to meet my brother!" and she cantered ahead, Stellar on her heels.

11

A HAPPY REUNION

As they reached the ash tree, they swivelled right and muscled through the bushes. When Stellar's sight was free from leaves, she blinked. A stubby white pony was nuzzling a pile of apples, and he had chocolate brown speckles on him, darker than Tallulah's. His mane was also rich and frizzy, but he had twigs sticking out of his hair and tail. He was also as skinny as the other wild horses, making him look even smaller than Stellar realised. She flicked her ear and guessed it was Peanut.

Chatting next to him was a leaner mare who was a very light grey, and she had black, sleek hair, and rare, green eyes. She had dark grey spots crowding her flank and across her cheeks like a wild storm. Stellar thought it was Demetra, the mare that Tallulah described Peanut had fallen in love with. Two foals scampered around the two: one pure, snow-white, and the other a light tan with a darker brown mane and white legs. Tallulah rushed towards Peanut.

"PEANUT!" Tallulah cried in joy. Before her brother could lift his head, he was flat on the ground with Tallulah twirling in circles around him. He staggered to his hooves and blinked. "Tallulah!" he neighed, and they both nuzzled each other on the snout.

"I haven't seen you in AGES," Tallulah huffed, and Stellar thought she saw a tear at her friend's eye. "Tallulah," Demetra smiled, and she touched Tallulah on the forehead with her muzzle. "It's nice to see you."

Then Tallulah looked at the foals scampering around. "Are those- "she gasped, and then Demetra and Peanut laughed. "No, no!" Demetra whinnied, "These are Alena and Bion. They are not our foals, but Harmonia's and Cadmus'. We are teaching them how to forage."

"To forage…" Stellar echoed, "sorry, what does that mean?"

Demetra looked at Stellar in surprise, as if she'd just noticed she was there. "To find the best scraps. Who are you?"

"I am Stellar," Stellar replied, "Tallulah's friend."

"Oh," Peanut glanced at her just once, and Stellar flattened her ears. She felt like she was in the wrong place, like a horse in a flock of pegasi. "But Alena and Bion aren't the only ones we're teaching today," Demetra added and beckoned to the trees beyond.

"Cecilia!" she neighed. A tiny, misty grey foal came scampering towards Demetra, her ears flat. She seemed to not know where she was galloping, for she was sniffing the air and stopping now and again.

Suddenly, Stellar noticed the foal's eyes. Cecilia's eyes were a milky blue with no pupil in the middle. This foal was blind.

"What's happening? I smell strangers!" Cecilia stuttered. Demetra nuzzled the foal on the forehead. "No, it's just us. Peanut's sister and her friend have come to visit." Cecilia swung her head around. Then her wide eyes stared cold at Stellar and Tallulah, as if seeing right through them. She turned her head back and trotted off with Alena and Bion.

"She was born with the blindness," Peanut explained, shaking his head sorrowfully. "But she knows no better. Seeing darkness is all she's ever known, and she's lived her best life, so far."

"Some of the other horses don't accept her," Demetra added, frowning, "They think that her blindness is a bad omen, and that she could be an ally of Brone.

They…they don't trust her."

"Oh," Stellar grunted, shifting weight from hoof to hoof. "I need to tell you something," all of them said in unison. Then they laughed. "You go first, Peanut," Tallulah whinnied.

"Humans are burning down the forest," Peanut's voice cracked.

12

A RISKY PLAN

After Peanut explained what had happened to the herd, it creepily matched Stellar's dream, and her predictions. "…they come in with these giant monsters that eat the earth," Demetra was saying. She shuddered. "They set our trees on fire…!"

"Well," Stellar interrupted. "A day ago, I had a dream about this herd. They were running through a forest that was on fire, and…and I think that was you."

"What a useful dream! Is that why you are here?" Demetra asked, shocked. Stellar and Tallulah nodded. "What was their name…" Tallulah murmured, and then she said, "Arcadia, right?"

"Yes," Peanut frowned.

"Is she sick from breathing in the smoke?" Tallulah questioned. Peanut nodded. "And Myra, but she is younger, and still has hope to fight it off."

"Is there any way we can help?" Stellar's ears flattened. "There must be a way. The humans have to stop!"

"Humans are humans," Demetra mumbled, looking at her hooves, "They will never stop until they get what they want."

"Not on my watch," Tallulah lashed her tail, scaring a curious squirrel. "We need to make a plan. At what time do the humans usually attack?"

"The afternoon," Peanut replied, "but it gets dark then. With autumn comes darkness early in the day." But Peanut was right. The sun was already setting on the horizon, even though it was just after midday. "I think I know who can help us cope with the darkness," Stellar realised. "Cecilia."

"What?" Demetra and Tallulah neighed. "She is just a foal," Tallulah protested. "And she must be kept with the other foals for safety," Demetra added.

"She is our only hope," Stellar pointed out, "the only one who is in darkness all the time. Tonight, or tomorrow night, we shall know how to move in the dark."

"I agree with Stellar," Peanut gruffed, "Cecilia will teach us well."

"W-what if it's not safe?" Demetra frowned. Stellar sighed, "None of this is safe."

"I've got a great idea," Tallulah butted in. "There will be four troops: one to attack the humans, one to stick sharp rocks and twigs into the tires of the monsters, one to care for the elderly and foals at camp, and one to put out the fires."

"That's great!" Stellar neighed. "But who will lead them?"

"Xanthia will lead the human-attacking patrol," Demetra decided. "She is great at fighting."

"Pyralis is fast," Peanut commented, "so he will lead the troop to attack the machines, and Agata for the fires."

"Apollo will stay with the eldest horses, and the foals," Demetra said, "he is strong and caring."

"It's decided, then?" Tallulah neighed.

"Yes," Demetra, Peanut and Stellar chorused. "Let's tell Cecilia."

13

MOMENTS BEFORE

"No," Cecilia shook her head, her wide, blank eyes staring sightlessly as the wild horses stumbled. They all had leaves flattened and wrapped over their eyes so they couldn't see. The wild horses felt around the floor desperately, neighing in alarm as they bumped into trees and each other.

"Scent the air. Feel the vibrations in the ground," Cecilia's voice soothed. The wild horses froze and started to sniff the whistling breeze. They shuffled their hooves. "This is useless!" a lean brown horse snapped. She lashed her tail. "Horses aren't built for the night. We're all going to burn in flames!"

A murmur of distress rippled over the horses. Cecilia lifted her head. "Maybe *you* will," Cecilia replied bravely,

"IF you don't believe in yourself, and your herd."

"But we will stand. We will let the moonlight guide us when midnight hits," Cecilia turned to a young, chocolate brown mare. "Kafe," she said, reaching out to the mare that nuzzled her behind the ear. "Tell your sister to calm down."

Kafe trotted up uneasily to the lighter brown mare and murmured something in her ear. Kafe's sister's ears perked up, and she sighed.

Cecilia started to stomp on the floor. The wild horses jumped in surprise. "Feel that?" Cecilia called. "This means danger. If you feel a vibration like this, that means the monsters are coming." The horses nodded eagerly. A few started to stomp as well.

Stellar stood next to Tallulah, nervous. The leaf wrap over her eyes blocked out everything except light. At night, she would see nothing. Blind or not, they would only see blackness.

They had been training for a while and the sun was below the horizon. As the herd removed the leaf wraps off their eyes one by one, the moon started to show behind the pine trees. Night-time.

Demetra trotted up behind Stellar and Tallulah. She had Xanthia at her side. "Get into your patrols!" Demetra demanded. The herd bustled and got into groups of fives. Xanthia started to set rules for her patrol.

A golden mare with white hair and dark blue eyes muscled through the crowd. It was Agata, the horse who would lead the patrol to stop the fires. She flickered her ear at several horses. "Come with me!" and they trotted off into the stretching shadows.

A big, light brown appaloosa horse flicked his ear. Apollo. "Ourania and Ophelos! Come with me, back to camp!" and they trailed after where Agata's patrol had disappeared.

As the herd separated into groups, Stellar shivered. "Will…will this work?" she murmured. Tallulah rubbed against Stellar's shoulder, gazing up at her warmly. "Of course, it will. You really are a great horse, Stellar. You're smart and you know what's right. The whole herd depends on us, now. We can't fail. We've got Amin with us."

As she spoke, Pyralis walked up to Tallulah. "Tallulah, you're small, and you won't be seen in the dark. You, Peanut, Nyx, Mathias, and I will attack the machines." Xanthia was at his side. She rested her icy gaze on Stellar. "You will join me, Leandros, Kronos and Jonas."

"I-I'm going to be in the *attacking* patrol?" Stellar gulped.

53

"Hm? Well, you can't just sit here and do nothing! Come on!" Xanthia snorted. As she fled, Stellar followed, along with a black and white stallion, a frosty, white with grey dappled stallion, and a caramel brown stallion.

14

THE HUMANS ATTACK

They stopped at the same stream Stellar and Tallulah had tripped over and fell in. Moonlight flickered on the surface of the cold, churning water, that snaked through the gloomy trees. She had so many questions but decided to keep quiet. Her heart was beating so fast, she thought it would jump out of her chest!

Suddenly, a monstrous, sparking flame licked and gobbled a tree. Stellar squealed in fright. "Agata should have her water supplies by now," Xanthia murmured.

"Erm- how exactly can she stop the fires?" Leandros the brown horse asked. Stellar couldn't tell Xanthia's expression in the darkness as she turned to face Leandros. "They soak moss in the river and squeeze the water onto the fires, to remove what helps fire burn things: heat."

"Smart," Kronos, the black and white stallion flicked his tail. "Aren't we going to do something?" Stellar fretted. Her hooves were tingling, and she wanted to smack her tail in the human's faces 1000 times. Xanthia detected Stellar's eagerness. "No. We need to find the humans first, of course. We need to surprise them."

"Jonas!" Xanthia ordered the grey and white dappled horse. "Take Kronos and go on each side of the humans. We are going to ambush them!"

Stellar thought about Tallulah and where she was right now. She thought about Arcadia, grasping onto her last string before it ripped and she tumbled over. And Cecilia, hanging back at camp with Apollo, blind and lost. Pyralis destroying the machines, Myra pleading for her sickness to go away, Peanut and Demetra, their dreams about future foals. The whole herd was at risk.

"Stellar!" Xanthia snapped. Her eyes were angry, but her tail was swaying anxiously. "I'll go distract the humans in front. Leandros will take you to surprise them behind."

Stellar nodded, and they separated. As Leandros and her cantered through the trees, they passed screeching oaks that toppled over, neighs of fear echoing in the forest. It was alive with fire now that munched and rolled into the forest like a hungry dog.

"Are we going to survive?" she found herself asking, and realised she'd said it aloud. Leandros gazed at Stellar. "I hope so. Amin might be running beside us right now. He'll make sure our herd lives for thousands of years, thriving in this ancient forest."

Stellar found herself glancing around, but there was no sign of a vanilla, muscular horse galloping alongside them.

They skidded to a halt and turned around. Stellar could spot big, sparkling yellow machines ripping trees from the soil ahead. Small silhouettes and shapes scuttled like beetles between the fire, some two-legged, furless bodies and other splodges that looked like horses. "How will we know when to attack?" Stellar grunted. Leandros shuffled his hooves. "Now!" he neighed.

They galloped forward at full speed and muscled through the humans. Heat licked at Stellar's flank as she passed, but she was too fast for the fire to catch on her mane or tail. She swerved around and reared onto two hooves at the humans. They wore white and yellow, baggy clothing and wearing black helmets. The humans chittered in surprise and shouted, then ran back to their machines. "Oh no you don't!" a voice neighed. It was Xanthia, chasing after the humans with her hair streaming out behind her. On either side of the sandy horse was Kronos and Jonas, and then Leandros, and lastly Stellar.

Together they chased away the humans as they slowly backed away. Suddenly, a stallion neighed in the darkness. It was Pyralis and his patrol, ready to attack the machines. They scored dents and scratches into the shiny, yellow pelts of the monsters.

15

THE FOREST OF FIRE

They kicked and shoved the machines and glass shattered on the ground. The humans leapt out of the big yellow monsters and screamed, retreating away into the night.

Agata and her patrol had cleared up most of the fires, and soon it was only the moonlight that lit Stellar's vision. For a while it was silent. The herd slowly came back together, emerging from the shadows of the trees, and flopping down exhausted on the ashes of the forest. Dust clogged in Stellar's nostrils and throat. She coughed, and then made sure not to breathe in any more smoke.

She lifted her head up. "We did it!" Stellar shouted. Neighs of delight and joy rose from the crowd. She hopped up onto a shaft of rock that struck from the ground, in the middle of the clearing. She gazed around. Most of the trees of the forest were burnt or crumbling away on the ground. Rubble and smoke billowed on the floor, and ashes littered the once perfectly green grass. The moon was full but clouded by smoke and clouds.

A cry of sorrow echoed from the back of the herd. Everyone turned around. A young horse lay on the ashes. Her peanut-butter brown flank did not rise. Her hazel eyes were clouded and her breath was stale. Over her crouched a shivering, dark brown mare. Kafe. And beside her sat a chestnut mare. Kafe's sister.

The herd gasped and crowded around the young mare that was now dead. "Give her some space!" Xanthia demanded. Stellar skidded down the rock and leapt at Kafe's side. The mare looked slowly up at Stellar, her eyes full of pain and tears rolling down her cheeks. Except this mare was looking up in hope. She had a new respect for Stellar now. "Wh-what do I do, Kosmos…" Kafe trembled, and she let out another cry of pain. "She was so young! Hebe!" she wailed out her little sister's name.

Stellar froze and looked down at Hebe. The tiny mare was still limp. It was too late to save her. Kosmos nuzzled Kafe's cheek. "She's in a better place now," the light brown horse breathed. Kafe fell silent, and for a few minutes the whole herd fell silent.

"What's happening?" Stellar whispered to Xanthia behind her. Xanthia whispered back, "It's a silence for the loss of Hebe. Every time a herd member dies, we are silent to think about her life and her dreams."

Stellar turned to gaze down at the mare. Suddenly a few wild horses got to their hooves and started to dig a hole. They dug it at the bottom of the rock and laid Hebe inside. Stellar watched as the mare was slowly engulfed by the freshest soil they could find. Kafe and her sister, Kosmos, laid buttercups on top of the grave.

Suddenly, Stellar spotted Tallulah, Peanut and Demetra among the crowd. She neighed in delight and bustled through the horses to get to her friend. When she did, she nuzzled Tallulah on the forehead. "You're here!" she cried.

"Of course, I am, stupid!" Tallulah snorted. "Now stop being dramatic and let's go home."

"Home?" Stellar asked. "Which home?"

"This home," Tallulah gestured to the fallen trees, the burnt grass, the shredded bushes, the smoky sky. "The forest of fire."

16

HOME

"These two domestic horses have worked hard to save our herd," Xanthia continued. She stood in front of some holly back at camp, whilst the herd crowded around Tallulah, Stellar and her. "They've made plans and they've risked their lives for us. For strangers, that they haven't even known until yesterday."

"Ahem," Peanut interrupted.

"Whatever," Xanthia snorted. "We owe them so much."

"We don't need anything," Tallulah smiled. "I believe we've already found what we want," and she nuzzled Peanut on the shoulder.

"Yes," Stellar added, feeling the fresh breeze of the slowly healing forest, the forest of fire. She could finally live as a wild horse. No humans, nothing, just the ancient trees and the grass underfoot.

"Sadly, we have lost a few horses in doing so," Demetra murmured. "We mourn the loss of Arcadia, Hebe and Evgenia to this day. But they are in a better place now. In a place where apples are infinite, and the skies are clear, safe with Amin. They will watch over our herd forever."

The herd murmured in agreement. Kafe lowered her head.

"Too many horses die young," Chara, the wisest horse, rasped.

"But with loss comes new life," Demetra added. "I proudly say that me and Peanut have had three foals!"

The herd cheered and whinnied in excitement.

Three foals stumbled up to Demetra and gazed around curiously. Two were a dappled brown colour like Peanut with green eyes like Demetra, and one white with grey dapples like Demetra and orange eyes, like Tallulah's. "Medeia, Melina and Pandora," she pointed to the foals affectionately. Bion shied up to the newborns. "Hi! I'm Bion!" he whinnied. Pandora, the grey-dappled foal gazed at him. "I'm Pandora. What's wrong with your snout?"

Bion screwed up his face in confusion.

"Enough wise talk," Xanthia called. "I think it's time these newcomers learn to be REAL wild horses."

"Hey!" Stellar protested sarcastically. "I'm AMAZING at apple-picking! Did you see the one I got this morning?"

"I'm pretty sure the herd wants no more brown apples for the day," Xanthia replied, smiling. Tallulah, Stellar and Xanthia laughed.

"Come on! Let's see what domestic horses can do," she smirked and galloped away. Tallulah followed with a protest. Stellar just snorted in amusement and trailed after.

And for a second, Stellar thought she had seen a vanilla horse with caramel hair. His flank glimmered as if it was made of crystal. He gazed at Stellar with frail, sky-blue eyes like sea glass.

"You've done well, my great granddaughter,"

and Amin was gone.

ABOUT THE AUTHOR

Blanca P. Mora Pratt is a ten-year-old Spanish/New Zealand girl living with her family and her dog, Grace the goldendoodle, in Cambridge, United Kingdom.

Reading and writing has always been part of Blanca's life. Influenced by Tui T. Sutherland, J.R.R. Tolkien, Erin Hunter and many more excellent writers, her love for literature has driven her to reach her goals: to finish her very first book.

Blanca is busy finishing off her final primary school years and is spending as much time with her friends as she can before she departs to secondary school and takes a leap out of her comfort zone.

Printed in Great Britain
by Amazon